WHO
IS THE
WORLD
FOR?

For Cameron and Jenny with all my love
and with special thanks to
Diana, Wendy and Lucy
T.P.

For Wendy
R.I.

First published 2000 by Walker Books Ltd
87 Vauxhall Walk, London SE11 5HJ

10 9 8 7 6 5 4 3 2 1

Text © 2000 Tom Pow
Illustrations © 2000 Robert Ingpen

This book has been typeset in Veljovic.

Printed in Belgium

British Library Cataloguing in Publication Data
A catalogue record for this book is available from the British Library.

ISBN 0-7445-6779-3

WHO IS THE WORLD FOR?

Written by TOM POW

Illustrated by ROBERT INGPEN

Walker Books
AND SUBSIDIARIES
LONDON · BOSTON · SYDNEY

Who is the world for?

the baby bear asks her mother
as she snuggles into her furry tummy
at the mouth of their winter cave.

Why, look around you,
the mother replies. The world
with all its deep dark caves
for you to shelter in, with all its
spring rivers, shining in sunlight,
shimmering with fish, and with all
its forests you'll never be lost in
no matter how very far they stretch ~

the world is for you!

Who is the world for?

the lion cub asks his father
as they lie together in the sun
and the father sniffs the dry, hot air.

Why, look around you, the father replies.

The world with all its grassy plains for you to run on,

with all its zebra and antelope and elephant for you to grow strong among

and with all its high smooth rocks for you to bask on ~

how can you doubt that

the world is for you!

Who is the world for?

the baby hippo asks his mother
as they lie together, so close in the water
their backs are like stepping stones.

Why, look around you, gurgles his mother.

    The world with all its wide, slow brown rivers for you to dance in,

and with all its deep muddy pools for you to wallow in, so cool

    in the midday sun even the elegant

antelope come down to drink ~

    the world is for you!

Who is the world for?

   the baby whale asks her mother
as they swim side by side
   like a tiny tug in the shadow
of an ocean liner.

Why, look around you,
    sings her mother. The world
with all its deep roomy seas for you
    to voyage through, all its million-kinded fish
that will part for you, all its rich seaweed,
    its watery lights, its sea sounds
    that speak so clearly to you ~

the world is for you!

Who is the world for?

the baby Arctic hare asks her father
as they cosy together from the wind
in a warm burrow of snow.

Why, look around you,
    her father replies. The world
with all its ice and snow will hide you
    and all its hidden green shoots
will feed you. Each day you will have a
    crisp white sheet to step out on, for

the white world is for you!

Who is the world for?

the baby owl asks his mother
as they sit side by feathery side
on a branch of sweet-smelling pine.

Why, look around you, his mother replies.

The world with all its high green trees for you to hoot from

and with all its fence posts for you to perch on, all its moonbeams

for you to swoop down on towards the tiniest rustling leaf ~

my dear, the world is a wood, and

the world is for you!

Who is the world for?

the small boy asks his father
as they kneel side by side
in a rumpled nest of blankets.

Why, the father replies,
the world is a very big place.

And somewhere under its stars ~

   way, way out there ~ on a cold mountainside,
bear cubs curl up beside their mothers in dark warm caves;
   lion cubs stretch out beside their fathers on a hot and dusty plain;
Arctic hares doze with slipper-soft babes in secret burrows of snow;
   and closer, much closer to home ~

listen! ~

an owl hoots to her baby from the
middle of the dark green wood.

The world is for
all of these.

The boy leans into his father,
as together they look out
into the big starry night.

And is the world for people too ~
like me and you? he asks.

Oh yes, answers his father,
wherever they may live,
the world is for people too.
The world is for everyone!

But **my** world is here ~ with you.
And **our** world has parks for you
to play in and rivers for you to cross.
It has hills for you to climb up high
and castles and seashores to explore.

Already we have seen so much
yet we've much, much more
to see and do.

Who is the world for?

The world is
for you!